For Benedict Bridgewood – much love J.W.

This paperback edition first published in 2020 by Andersen Press Ltd.
First published in Great Britain in 2007 by Andersen Press Ltd., 20 Vauxhall Bridge Road, London SW1V 2SA.
Text copyright © Jeanne Willis, 2007. Illustrations copyright © Tony Ross, 2007.
The rights of Jeanne Willis and Tony Ross to be identified as the author and illustrator of this
work have been asserted by them in accordance with the Copyright, Designs and Patents Act, 1988.
All rights reserved. Colour separated in Switzerland by Photolitho AG, Zürich.
Printed and bound in Malaysia.

2   4   6   8   10   9   7   5   3   1

British Library Cataloguing in Publication Data available.

ISBN 978 1 83913 002 1

This book belongs to:

. . . .

Cottonwool COLIN

Jeanne Willis and Tony Ross

Andersen Press • London

Once, there were ten baby mice.

For mice, they were BIG and **bold** and bouncy.

All except for Colin.

Colin was the smallest of mice.

He was very, very small.

Even for a mouse.

His mother didn't worry about
his brothers, or his sisters.
They were big enough
to look after themselves.

But she worried about Colin Smally.
She was afraid he might get hurt.
She made him sit indoors quietly.

She wouldn't
let him climb.

Or run.

Or jump.

In case he fell.

He couldn't go out in spring – in case he got wet.
Or summer – in case he got hot.
Or autumn – in case a chestnut fell on his head.

By winter, Colin was bored.
He wanted to go out into the BIG
w–i–d–e world. But his mother said,
"No, the world is too big and too wide
for you, Smally."
"You wrap Colin up in cotton wool,"
said his Grandma.

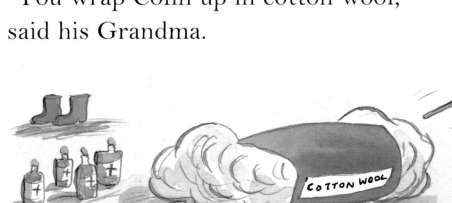

"What a good idea!" thought his mother.
And that's exactly what she did.

She wrapped him up.

Round and round and round,

so only his feet stuck out.
He was Cottonwool Colin.

At last, he was allowed out,
all wrapped up in cotton wool,
safe from rain and sun and snow.

If he fell, he would have a soft landing.
If anything fell on him, he wouldn't feel it.
He was as safe as safe could be... or was he?

"Oh look, a *snowball!*" laughed a little boy.
He picked Colin up and threw him...
SPLOSH! Into the f..f..freezing river.

Some of Colin's cotton
wool came off.
"Oh look, a meringue!"
quacked a duck.

And it chased him – Peck! Peck! Peck!
More cotton wool came off.
Colin swam and swam.
He climbed onto the bank, all bedraggled.

"Oh look, a fat white rabbit!" said the hungry fox.
And it chased him – Snap! Snap! Snap!
All the cotton wool came off.

Colin ran and ran.
He jumped down a hole.
And hid.

The fox went away.

Colin Smally
dried out in the sun.
He skipped back home,
feeling very LARGE.

His mother was horrified.
"Colin, where is your cotton wool?"
she shrieked. "Anything could have
happened to you!"

"Everything *did* happen to me,"
he whooped.

I got pecked.

"I got wet. I got cold.

But I swam

I got chased.

and I ran

and I jumped and...

Mama, I'm *alive!*

I survived without my cotton wool!
May I go out to play again tomorrow?"
His mother took a deep breath
and said...

"Yes. If you must.
Take care. Take a coat. Be good.
Have fun. Love you, Smally."

Colin went out into the world.
Sometimes he got scared
and sometimes he got hurt.

But ohhhhhh... it was worth it!

Other books by
Jeanne Willis and Tony Ross:

Hippospotamus

Slug Needs a Hug

Daft Bat

Misery Moo

Boa's Bad Birthday

The T-Rex Who Lost His Specs!

The Pet Person

Old Dog

Big Bad Bun